The Extraordinary Lives of Ordinary People

Gauri Jhangiani is a young author with a zest for both writing and life. When she's not writing, she enjoys reading, binge-watching TV shows and spending many hours on Tumblr. *The Extraordinary Lives of Ordinary People* is her first book.

The Extraordinary Lives of Ordinary People

Gauri Jhangiani

RUPA

Published by
Rupa Publications India Pvt. Ltd 2016
7/16, Ansari Road, Daryaganj
New Delhi 110002

Sales Centres:

Allahabad Bengaluru Chennai
Hyderabad Jaipur Kathmandu
Kolkata Mumbai

Copyright © Gauri Jhangiani 2016

All rights reserved.
No part of this publication may be reproduced, transmitted,
or stored in a retrieval system, in any form or by any means,
electronic, mechanical, photocopying, recording or otherwise,
without the prior permission of the publisher.

This is a work of fiction. Names, characters, places and incidents are
either the product of the author's imagination or are used fictitiously and
any resemblance to any actual person, living or dead,
events or locales is entirely coincidental.

ISBN: 978-81-291-3736-4

First impression 2016

10 9 8 7 6 5 4 3 2 1

The moral right of the author has been asserted.

Printed by Replika Press Pvt. Ltd., India

This book is sold subject to the condition that it shall not,
by way of trade or otherwise, be lent, resold, hired out, or otherwise circulated,
without the publisher's prior consent, in any form of binding or cover other than
that in which it is published.

For Hannah.
I will remember you—always.

Contents

Jolly Holiday	1
Felix	11
Vichyssoise	19
Secrets	27
Radar	37
Best Friends Forever	45
The Conversation	55
Diamond in the Rough	59
Thoughts	67
Prized Possessions	75
The Games People Play	81
A Match Made in Heaven	91
Partners	99
Acknowledgements	111

Jolly Holiday

'Excuse me, can you help me?' Nina asked a passer-by. 'I'm looking for India Gate.'

The man frowned.

'Madam, it's right down the road, in fact you can see it from here,' he replied curtly before walking on.

Nina looked in the direction he had pointed and was not disappointed at all. India Gate was in sight and it was beautiful. Although Nina was an Indian who had lived in India all her life, she had never had a chance up until now to explore Delhi and its treasures—including the one in front of her. She was feeling excited as she hurried on in the direction of India Gate, dragging her little suitcase behind her.

When she finally made it to the monument, she spent time she didn't actually have admiring it. The stone arch stood tall and proud and even from a distance she could clearly read the tiny inscriptions—recognition to those who had sacrificed themselves for their country. Braving the crowds, Nina walked closer to India Gate and examined the Amar Jawan Jyoti, an eternal fire, also in commemoration of the brave. She was completely enthralled by everything in the area, from the dirty pond nearby, where children and adults rowed in paddle boats, to the peddlers trying to sell a variety of useless goods, and of course, the monument itself.

While Nina haggled with a vendor over a colourful night light, she felt someone tap her shoulder and found an exasperated taxi driver standing behind her.

'Nina Madam!' he exclaimed. 'I have been searching all over for you. I am the driver from the guest house. I'll take you to the Innova...you are Nina Madam, right?'

'Yes,' an amused Nina answered, 'hold on a minute.'

Nina quickly paid the vendor the money he had asked for, without any further argument, and followed the driver. The peddler was delighted with how easily she had given in to his demands. He had made a good first sale of the day.

Meanwhile, the harried driver escorted Nina to the car and plopped her tiny suitcase into the boot. Nina settled herself comfortably in the back seat and they took off as she watched the sights go by.

When they reached the guest house, Nina was surprised to find the owner waiting for her. Nina recognized her from the photo on her website, a horrible and unflattering portrait of a woman who was short, stout and middle-aged.

'Hello,' the owner greeted her, 'I am Abha, the owner of Paradise Guest House.'

'Yes,' Nina smiled, 'I know who you are, your photo was on the interspace.'

'The what?' Abha asked, puzzled.

'The interspace.'

'Oh!' Abha exclaimed. 'I think you mean the internet! My son taught me about that.'

'Yes, sorry. I meant the internet. I'm terribly scatter-brained today,' Nina apologized.

'Don't worry, my dear!' the genial Abha replied. 'Truth be told, if anyone should be sorry it's us.'

She led Nina into the reception-cum-living room, where Nina signed in the guestbook. Abha called for an attendant to check whether Nina's room was ready. In the meanwhile, Abha decided that if there was any time to apologize profusely for the inconvenience she had caused, it was now.

'I'm terribly sorry, Nina. I thought your flight was coming in later.'

'It's all right, Abha. Accidents happen.'

'Yes, but I feel horrible about not having sent the car on time and leaving you stranded at the airport. My driver should have taken you to India Gate.'

'As I had told you over the phone, Abha, there's no harm done and in fact if a driver wasn't included in your package, I wouldn't have hired one separately. I have a very small suitcase and it's very easy to carry around. What I don't have, though, is time. If I had that, I would have waited at the airport. The next flight back home is tomorrow, so I can't waste a single minute.'

Seeing Abha's worried face, Nina added, 'But don't worry, you didn't waste any of my time. I spent it fruitfully at India Gate.'

'Well, I'm glad,' Abha said, brightening up, 'but why aren't you staying longer? You live in Mumbai, there are flights every day. Twenty-four hours is too little to see the city.'

'My favourite airline has these awkward timings, so I'm bound to them,' Nina replied.

The conversation was interrupted by the appearance of the attendant who announced that 'Nina Madam's room' was ready for her.

Nina went upstairs and found her suitcase already in her room. She pulled out some fresh clothes and had a quick bath. Ten minutes later, she was ready to leave.

'My dear, you are fast,' Abha exclaimed when Nina reappeared in the reception-cum-living room. 'The driver is ready for you.'

Nina hopped into the car and instructed the driver to take her to Qutab Minar. As they drove along, she took out a notebook from her rucksack and turned the pages to a list of monuments she wanted to see that day:

India Gate
Qutab Minar
Humayun's Tomb
Lotus Temple
Jama Masjid

She quickly updated her list by crossing off the first item. She considered whether she would have time for anything else and after much deliberation (the whole journey), concluded she would not. Feeling both disappointed and elated—the former due to lack of time and the latter because of what she was going to see—Nina entered the Qutab Minar complex.

It was a weekday, and hence the place was crawling with schoolchildren, but Nina didn't mind. In fact, she adored them. However, her attention was focused on the massive tower in front of her.

'Wow,' she murmured.

She went as close to it as she possibly could and strained her neck to see the top of the tower. It truly was huge and wonderful with beautiful carvings on its asymmetrical body, unlike anything Nina had ever seen. However, she did not have the time to gaze at it forever and she briskly moved on to view the rest of the complex, including the famed iron pillar.

Nina's next stop at Humayun's Tomb also enchanted

her. The final resting place of the noble king in a tomb of mellow red sandstone appealed to her and she hoped in vain that she could be buried in a similarly gorgeous place.

Nina then headed to the Lotus Temple, where the concept of praying inside confused her, as she had been an atheist all her life. Walking barefoot on the ground outside was similar to dancing on hot coals, but overall, Nina enjoyed herself.

After the sun had set, Nina visited Jama Masjid. She admired its architecture and explored Chandni Chowk. She loved how vibrant the shops were and how wonderful the street food was. When purchasing a lehenga from one of the stores, Nina made sure to haggle properly this time and was elated when her efforts paid off. Finally, she ate dinner in McDonald's.

Nina was pleased at the status of her list. It now showed:

~~India Gate~~
~~Qutab Minar~~
~~Humayun's Tomb~~
~~Lotus Temple~~
~~Jama Masjid~~

She smiled.

The next morning she packed her few belongings into her miniature suitcase and went out to the car. Abha was outside, waiting to bid her goodbye, all the while apologizing for the blunder with the car.

When Nina reached the airport, she quickly passed through security and went towards the airport lounge for privileged passengers. The departure time for her flight being some time away, she pulled out her laptop and started watching a movie. About an hour later, there was an announcement.

'Ladies and gentlemen, please hold on to your belongings and make sure that you are far apart from any other passengers.'

Then the entire lounge rotated 180 degrees, and the passengers landed on plush, cushioned mattresses below. Nearby, a high-tech lift pinged. From it emerged a single elderly person in a wheelchair. On the other end of the underground area another lift pinged. There were eight such lifts, each having the capacity to carry only one person. Once all the passengers had retrieved their belongings, they formed an orderly queue next to the mattresses. 'Right, please follow me, passengers,' an airhostess announced.

She led everyone further underground through a tunnel. The tunnel eventually led to a bunker, where a massive jet thrummed and the ground staff carried out final checks.

'You may enter, passengers. Welcome aboard,' the airhostess said amiably, opening the doors to the jet.

Nina headed inside and settled in her seat. A few minutes later an old lady occupied the seat next to her.

She folded away her walker and settled back. Something about her seemed familiar to Nina. However, she could not put her finger on what exactly it was.

'So,' the old lady croaked, 'what brings you to 2015?'

'I just wanted to see New Delhi in its full glory,' Nina answered with a smile. 'It did not disappoint!'

'I'm glad,' the elderly woman said. 'I'm Abha, by the way.'

Nina was astounded.

'Did you own a guest house?'

'At one time, yes,' the old lady said wistfully. 'But why do you ask?'

'My name's Nina. I just stayed there.'

'Well then, Nina, you know how beautiful it was before the fall of the city.'

'Indeed it was.'

Abha sighed. 'It's sad to watch the things you love being ruined. I know my younger self will find it hard tomorrow. Well, at least we get these occasional time trips so that we can see the former glory of New Delhi.'

'That's true,' Nina said sadly. 'We didn't know what we had, till it was gone.'

Another announcement came over the speaker.

'Ladies and gentlemen, Time Airways flight number B221 is ready for take-off. Please fasten your seatbelts as the journey through hyperspace may be bumpy. We will reach our destination in approximately five minutes.'

They had barely taken off when another announcement was made, 'Ladies and gentlemen, welcome to the year 2100.'

Felix

It was definitely not Aditya's day. He had accidentally ruined a crucial meeting and his boss had yelled at him. The only upside was that he hadn't been fired. However, he felt that a particularly hard day at work did warrant that he spend time at a bar, drowning his sorrows in alcohol, in the company of strangers. So he took a cab to an out-of-the-way pub where the chances of bumping into someone he knew were low and yet they mixed a good drink. He plonked himself on a bar stool and ordered the best whisky they had.

As he contemplated his woes, another man sat down beside him and ordered the same drink. The new arrival was attired in a dark and worn-out overcoat, under which was an equally shabby suit and tie. His hair was raven-black and pulled back in what the fashion world called a 'man bun'. Aditya noted that although the man's general appearance was forlorn, it was offset by the stark white trainers he wore. They looked expensive and brand new. In fact, it was this very oddity in the newcomer's appearance that started a conversation between them.

The stranger noticed Aditya's fleeting glances at his shoes and said, 'They're from my first pay cheque.'

Aditya pretended that he hadn't been looking. He wasn't really in the habit of conversing with unknown people, or known ones for that matter.

'Oh really?' he asked.

'Yes,' the stranger continued, 'I am a writer, but it's only now that my first novel has been published. The first thing I wanted to do was to buy new shoes, so here they are.'

Aditya, an avid reader, was greatly intrigued by writers. He had heard many authors talk about their profession, but until that moment, had never met one in the flesh. His desire to learn more overcame his initial unfriendliness as he eagerly asked questions about the novel.

'Your novel, what's it about?'

'Well,' the stranger began, 'it's a bizarre murder mystery which leaves everybody stumped, except for my detective-protagonist, of course.'

'That sounds interesting. What's the case?'

'If I tell you that, my book sales will plummet.' The stranger laughed heartily and Aditya grinned too.

'So,' Aditya asked, 'if you've published a novel, then

what are you doing here?'

'I can't enjoy a drink?' the stranger asked, a faint smile playing on his lips.

'No, by all means, please do.'

Aditya paused to clink his glass with the stranger; the other downed his drink in one clean swig and had the bartender refill it.

'But given your success, why would you want to come to this out-of-the-way bar, and not a better and trendier one?'

The stranger averted his gaze. The question evidently bothered him. Aditya, noticing his discomfort, proceeded to apologize for his impertinence, but the stranger cut him off with two little words: 'writer's block'. He looked down at his glass before turning to Aditya, who was amazed that a hurdle in the creative process could make one resort to alcohol for help.

'My friend,' the stranger began, 'I am an author and I have penned a book, it is true. But now my publisher has put pressure on me to deliver another book. He wants me to make it into a series. I wanted to write a different type of book, but he wouldn't agree. He told me to write the sequel or I'd have to find another publisher. I only intended to make my detective solve one case. Now *he* wants him to solve more.'

The stranger looked so distressed that Aditya had to ask, 'Is there any way I can help?'

The stranger mournfully shook his head.

'Unless you can conjure up a way for the victim to die, I'm afraid not.'

'I'm not so bad at thinking up stories,' Aditya said. 'Why don't we try together?'

'All right,' the stranger replied, 'as long as you don't steal the story for yourself, I guess it wouldn't hurt. My detective's name is something else, but everyone calls him Felix. Felix has to investigate the death of his long-lost cousin. Essentially, he has a personal connection with the victim, but only becomes aware of their relationship during the course of the investigation. However, the real dilemma is killing the victim. I need an interesting method of homicide. I refuse to use run-of-the-mill methods like guns and knives. Now you tell me, how should I kill him so that the crime piques Felix's interest?'

Aditya pondered over this for a minute or so.

'Have you decided who the murderer will be?' he inquired.

'Yes.'

'Is the killer Felix's friend or foe?'

'I probably shouldn't be telling you this, but neither; he is going to be a policeman with an agenda that has nothing to do with Felix.'

'Is that wise?'

'Well, I do have an entire franchise to introduce Felix's greatest nemeses.'

Aditya tried not to grin.

'That does sound good. So can you tell me the agenda?'

'No, I can't tell you more, but from the information I have shared, what do you think I should do with the victim? I need a completely unique cause of death.'

'Have you considered a cricket bat? Or even missiles? No, forget the missiles. No policeman has access to missiles. Let me think...'

Aditya considered all the possibilities. Never had he so desperately thought of ways to kill someone. In order to get his creative juices flowing, he began to visualize himself as the murderer, standing over the dead body of the victim, who bore a suspicious resemblance to his tyrant boss.

'How about gutting the victim and spreading out his innards in a shape of some significance?'

'I don't think that will fit.'

'What about a postcard?'

'Death by paper-cut is not very inspiring.'

Finally, the stranger got up. He looked exhausted.

'I'm sorry, but none of your ideas seem to do the trick. Maybe I will succeed tomorrow.'

He turned to leave.

'WAIT!' Aditya called out. 'I have something!'

The stranger stopped dead in his tracks.

'Well,' Aditya began tentatively. 'Your killer could

use an icicle. An icicle is sharp and can cause fatal wounds. When it melts, it becomes untraceable. It makes for a fantastic case as the murder weapon would have disappeared. Only your detective will be smart enough to consider the possibility of such a bizarre murder weapon.'

The stranger was dumbstruck.

'Wow!' he exclaimed. 'Just wow! That's amazing! This idea would never have occurred to me! I will definitely use your cause of death in my story.'

He rose to leave and paused.

'By the way, why are *you* at the bar?' he asked.

Aditya smiled. The incident with his boss seemed like a long time ago.

'My reasons for being here are far too mundane. They will bore you,' he finally answered.

'I assure you they will not. Now please do tell.'

'I'm here because…my boss yelled at me. I screwed up a crucial meeting.'

'Oh,' the other said, 'if it's any consolation, Felix got fired from his detective agency.'

Aditya grinned.

'I'm terribly sorry I never introduced myself properly,' he said to the stranger. 'My name is Aditya Pillai.'

'Nice to meet you Aditya, I'm Vir Roy,' the stranger replied.

Both of them shook hands briefly before Vir took his leave. After that, Aditya finished his drink and headed home. As he travelled in the cab, he marvelled at the fact that on the same day he had both ruined and fixed two different things.

'Aaaggh,' Aditya groaned, as he woke up the next morning clutching his aching head.

Last night's drinking had not gone down well with him and what was more, he still had to go to work and face his mean boss. He shuddered just at the thought of it. As he left the house, he picked up the newspaper. Sitting in the bus, he glanced through the articles dispassionately. It was the usual mix—dirty politics, rising crime and more studies linking lifestyle to diseases, but it was an article on page 3 that caught Aditya's attention. As he read it carefully, his face turned a pale shade of white. He suddenly felt nauseated and quickly de-boarded the bus and ran home, throwing the newspaper in a nearby dustbin. It sat there sadly, bearing the headlines 'Novelist found dead with big gaping hole in his chest, cause of death unknown.' It went on to describe the victim as one Vir Roy, who was discovered in a pool of his own blood. His death had baffled the police as no murder weapon was found. However, part of a manuscript was discovered in a puddle nearby, the last sentence unfinished. It read, 'Felix slowly picked up what he considered to be an ideal murder weapon—an ici-'

Vichyssoise

It was pouring cats and dogs when I left work that day. It was a Wednesday, I think. Yes, a Wednesday, that miserable day sandwiched between the dreadful Monday and Tuesday and the 'all right' Thursday and Friday, which ultimately gave way to what I hoped would be a glorious weekend. It was raining and I was driving home when I saw a short man sticking out his thumb. For some reason I felt sorry for him and let him into my car.

The previous week, I had gone to see a fortune-teller. I'd had a specific question to ask, which was of supreme importance to me.

'Madam,' I had begun carefully, 'I have had a dream for a while. I have always wanted to own a restaurant. Specifically, I have wanted a restaurant where I can serve people fantastic gourmet food. You know, vichyssoise and the rest.'

The word 'vichyssoise' was met with a blank stare.

'Cold soup?' I tried.

I received the same response.

'Oh, never mind!' I cried, throwing my hands in the air in exasperation. 'That was not my point. My point is that I have wanted a restaurant for a while. I made the down payment on a nice little place, but now I've had to scrap that plan because the place caught fire. I got my money back, but I want to know whether it is in my future or not to live my dream.'

The fortune-teller nodded and then gazed deep into the crystal ball before closing her eyes and then looking back at me.

'It seems to be in your future,' she announced with a dreamy smile, 'all you have to do is to be patient and believe. Your actions will soon be rewarded.'

Well, I'd wanted to know about my future and I had, but I really should have realized that the fortune-teller would only give me the answer I wanted to hear. 'Believe?' What kind of crap answer was that? The fortune-teller seemed to have mistaken herself for some type of fairy godmother.

Anyway, for reasons unknown, that particular conversation was playing in my head over and over again when I picked up the man.

'Hello!' he said smiling brightly. 'I'm really glad you saved me from the rain.'

'Look man,' I said curtly, 'I will drop you off at the nearest bus stop or train station or whatever, but I can't drop you off at your doorstep. Also, can you please sit at the back?'

'No problem!' the man replied, an unwavering grin plastered on his face.

'All right then, where do you need to be dropped off?'

'Not too far away. In fact if you keep going straight, you'll hit it.'

'Okay, then I guess I can drop you off.'

'Glad to hear that.'

We drove on through the busy streets while the stranger tried to make small talk.

'So, where are you from?'

'This city.'

'What is your favourite band?'

'Maroon 5.'

'What do you do?'

'I'm an architect.'

'That must be fascinating.'

'Not really. I do just about the same stuff that all architects do.'

After a while the man gave up trying to talk to me.

'Keep driving straight,' he told me.

I did so. I was still wondering why the fortune-teller's words were coming back to me, when I suddenly realized that we had left the city behind and I was now driving through forestland.

'Are you sure this is the right way?' I asked nervously. 'You don't live in a cabin in the woods, do you?'

'No,' the man answered.

I sneaked a quick glance at him through the rear mirror. He didn't look as jolly as before; maybe he understood that I didn't want to talk to him. Whatever it was, I drove on.

Soon it began to get darker and now, despite being a grown man, I was starting to worry. We had been driving for at least forty-five minutes. Enough, I decided and stopped the car.

'Why are you stopping?' the stranger asked.

'I'm stopping because I don't know where I'm going! We're practically in the countryside!'

'But it's right near here,' the stranger protested.

'Are you sure about that? Because I have been driving for forty-five minutes and there is nothing in sight! Get out!'

At that moment, a police car that had been cruising along pulled over on the side of the road and two cops came to investigate.

'Is everything all right?' a cop asked.

'This is between me and him,' I faltered, noticing that the cop was aiming his gun at me.

His partner was opening the car door and reaching for the whimpering little man in the back seat. He yanked the stranger out of my car and then ordered me to get out too. I did so, slowly and carefully, my eyes fixed on the gun. It looked nothing like the regular guns cops carried in our city. This looked more like something I would see in a mafia-spy-ring movie! Something told me these guys weren't real cops at all. Their shoes looked too expensive to belong to cops.

'We'll be taking him,' one of the guys snarled as he forced the terrified little man into the back seat of their car.

'But why?' I stuttered foolishly.

Both the men howled with laughter.

'Maybe our boss will keep you around for amusement's sake,' the taller of the two answered. 'Now get in the car.'

'Wait!' I cried as they pushed me into the car. 'I don't know anything! I'm just a regular person!'

'Sure,' one of the fake policemen scoffed, 'the getaway driver is always innocent.'

They stuffed me in the back seat with the stranger and tied our hands up. Just as they were about to get into the car, a cell phone rang. Both of them stood outside, having a long, angry conversation with whoever was on the phone.

'What did you do to upset them?' I hissed angrily at the man next to me.

He looked miserable.

'Something I shouldn't have done. I also shouldn't have brought you into the middle of this.'

'No shit. But why are they out to get you?'

'They are drug dealers and I stole from them. But I had to do it; I needed the drugs for my wife. She is dying and I don't have the money for her surgery. My cousin is a dealer so I fleeced drugs off these guys to sell it to him. Now, I won't make it in time. I'll die and so will my wife.'

He started to cry.

Up until now, I had been told I had a cold heart. Hell, up until now I had been very unfriendly with this guy, who had in fact *used* me. And now, despite everything, I wanted to help him.

'I'll get you to your cousin,' I said confidently.

Glancing around, I realized that we needed a miracle to get our hands free. I told the man to use the seatbelt buckle to cut the ties. Luckily, the buckle was sharp enough to cut through our bonds. Suddenly, the men came back to the car.

'Get to the front,' I whispered to the stranger next to me.

I attacked the man who was getting into the front seat and grabbed his gun. Using it, I shot him and the other man, but not before I was hit. The bullet pierced my chest. The last thing I saw was my companion climbing over the seats.

I awoke suddenly. Everything around me was blurry at first, but then, as things came into focus, I realized I was in a restaurant booth.

'W-what?' I cried, feeling utterly bemused.

'Oh good, sir, you're awake,' a voice said.

I saw a man half my size, standing in front of me.

'What am I d-doing here?' I stuttered.

'This is your restaurant sir,' the man said, beaming at me. 'Welcome to Heaven's Kitchen.'

As I looked around closely, I realized that the restaurant was full. There were many similarly short people who were serving food and I realized that the man in front of me was a waiter. He led me to the kitchen, which smelt wonderful. What I beheld was beautiful: the most well-stocked and busy kitchen I had ever seen, with the staff comprising short people who were happily preparing beautiful dishes.

'This is all m-mine?' I asked the waiter.

'Yes sir, your brave actions were rewarded.'

I was immediately reminded of the fortune-teller's words. All I had to do was be patient and believe.

'What's that?' I asked, pointing to what looked like dishwater in a bowl.

'Vichyssoise,' the waiter answered.

'Well, you're doing it wrong,' I said knowledgeably and proceeded to fix the soup.

I was finally living the dream. Even if it was in the afterlife.

Secrets

She took a deep breath before pushing open the gigantic double doors and entering the backstage area. She tried to quell the rising tide of excitement building up inside her, but then again, it wasn't every day that you met your favourite band, even if you were a journalist.

'Be professional,' she told herself nervously before smoothing her skirt and sitting on a chair.

It was some time before a suavely dressed man appeared in front of her and introduced himself as the band manager. As they walked to the dressing room, he told her that he had never heard of her magazine.

'It's okay,' she replied, 'most people haven't, but it is fairly up-and-coming and it'll be well-known very soon.'

'Yes, I suspect you will be the one to make it famous.'

The optimism of his words didn't match the look on his face.

'Thank you,' was all she could say.

'Exactly how old are you?' he asked.

'I am twenty-eight.'

'All right, if you say so,' the man said, not looking even remotely convinced.

She didn't care though. Youth didn't have to act as a hindrance in the pursuit of excellence and a career.

From inside the dressing room, the soft melody of an acoustic guitar signalled that the band was inside and waiting. The manager slipped inside and immediately the music stopped. After a minute, he re-emerged.

'You can go in now,' he said flatly.

Taking a deep breath, she walked in.

'Hello,' she managed, 'I'm from *Tunes Magazine* and I'm here to interview you all.'

'We're...'

'Yes, I know who you are.'

'Then let's begin.'

As she looked through her bag to pull out her trusty notebook and pen, she watched the four out of the corner of her eye. Young and stylish was the best way to describe them; in that manner, they were unanimously glamorous. However, that was the only characteristic they shared— each eighteen-year-old boy was completely different from the other.

The first was the boy who had spoken. He was the frontman and the leader (not to mention the only one who could still have a career if the band ever broke up). He had sandy blond hair in perfectly defined curls and piercing blue eyes. From the videos she had seen, she knew that when he laughed those eyes would light up accompanied by a radiant smile.

The second was skinny as a stick. He was probably the most dressed up for a magazine interview (where his appearance did not matter). While the others lounged about in sweatpants and tank tops, he sat in front of her in a formal shirt and trousers, constantly tapping his feet. His hair was messy, but in a very deliberate and stylish way. His dark eyes exuded nervousness. The only thing that seemed to be keeping him from exploding was the maroon bass guitar plastered with stickers that he was plucking.

The third one seemed somewhat intimidating. He hunched forward, his eyes trained on her, watching intently, as if he was trying to figure her out. His sturdy frame was much broader than the others and his coiffed black hair had red streaks.

The fourth boy was the one who puzzled her the most. In all the interviews that she had seen of them, never once had he answered any question with anything more than a simple 'yes' or 'no'. Even now, he didn't look like he intended to say much—it was evident on his face and in his quiet demeanour. He rarely ever smiled and never bothered to dress up or down. Like any other day, he was wearing his standard uniform of black jeans and a band t-shirt today. He looked extremely bored, like he couldn't wait to finish the interview and send her packing. Although all the boys were good-looking, there was something about this one that made him seem the most handsome.

After finally locating her journalistic tools of the trade, she started off with her interview.

'So, it's been just a few months since you announced your first tour. What do you have in mind for your fans?'

The sandy-haired boy immediately perked up.

'We have tons planned! It's going to be like nothing you've ever seen before! We'll obviously have the music, fireworks and fun, but we'll also probably have some flamethrowers.'

She raised an eyebrow at him.

'No kidding! Come on, boys, tell her!'

The others immediately backed him up vociferously. Except for the fourth boy, of course. 'Can you tell me anything else?'

'We can't divulge all the juicy details, sweetheart,' Sandy-Hair said, winking at her.

'Are you working on any new material currently?'

'Oh yeah, we're always in the studio, recording,' the third boy answered.

She glanced over at the fourth boy. He was busy texting on his phone.

'Anyway, moving on, how close are you as a band?'

'We're extremely close,' Sandy-Hair explained. 'We're a group of guys, we love music and we love gir...I mean our fans of course! Don't write the "girls" part. We also have secret talents!'

At that moment, professionalism went out of the window for the journalist.

'What secret talents?' she asked, grinning wickedly.

'Wait,' the nervous boy said, 'you're not going to write about this, are you?'

'Not if you don't want me to.'

'Well,' the third boy piped up, 'I, for one, am okay with telling you my secret talent and I hope...' he paused to give the others a meaningful look, 'that they are too. However, I have one condition.'

'Name it.'

'You have to tell us your secrets.'

A smirk appeared on his smug face. Immediately, the others also began to insist on the stipulation and the journalist had no choice but to agree.

'Okay, okay! I'll do it! Just know that this isn't part of my regular job description.'

They all laughed at this. Even Mystery Boy.

'I'll go first,' Sandy-Hair exclaimed.

'Of course you will,' said the third one, grinning.

She mentally labelled him 'Mind-Reader' for the way he kept trying to read her and search her soul.

'We-ell,' Sandy-Hair practically sang, 'my secret talent is that I style other people's hair.'

'That's hardly a secret,' she said, trying to hide her disappointment. 'You have perfectly done curls.'

As soon as she realized what she had said, her cheeks flushed and she noticed the other boys give her a strange look.

'What I meant to say was that…it's pretty evident that you style them.'

'I like that I have this effect on girls. Especially a pretty one like you,' he said before winking at her.

She looked away, goosebumps rising on her arms.

'Hey, he styles my hair everyday,' Mystery Boy said enthusiastically.

'Okay, what about you now?' she gestured to Nervous Boy.

'I-I-I just sort of…'

'Spit it out!' Sandy-Hair cried.

'Okay, fine! I can fit about ten packets' worth of gummy bears in my mouth! There, I freakin' said it!'

'Really?' she asked, completely stunned.

'Yes.'

His face now took on an expression of intense disgust and he suddenly seemed distinctly hostile.

'What, you thought that because I'm skinny and I have this nervous air around me I must be anorexic? That I never pig out? That I never have fun and only starve myself!?'

'Chill,' Mind-Reader said calmly, gently patting his friend on the back, 'it's an impossible feat for most. She didn't mean to be rude.'

Nervous Boy relaxed a bit.

'I'm sorry. I didn't mean to get upset. It's just…I'm very sensitive about such things…'

'No, no. It's fine.'

'My turn, right,' Mind-Reader started off. 'I have an immediate instinct about whether or not to trust someone.'

'And?' she pushed.

'You seem to have passed my test, but barely.'

She frowned.

'You seem to be a nice girl, but you are ambitious, which does not make you 100 per cent trustworthy,' he explained.

'Ambition is that bad?'

'No, not really. Although sometimes it makes people change. Do things that are not like them. Like you.'

With that, he bored his dark eyes into her, searching her soul.

'Right,' Mystery Boy rubbed his hands together. 'I used to love playing with Barbie dolls when I was younger. I learned my secret talent of being fantastic at fashion from them.'

'No!' Sandy-Hair gasped dramatically.

'Excuse me,' Mind-Reader said, clearly miffed, 'we've never heard this before.'

'Never thought to mention it before,' Mystery Boy shrugged.

Now they all looked at her meaningfully.

'I don't have a secret talent, but I do have a secret. I've never been to college,' she announced.

That truly shocked them.

'How can you be a professional journalist without having gone to college?!' Sandy-Hair screamed.

'I'll explain in the next round.'

The game proceeded into the next round. Sandy-Hair revealed that despite being the pretty boy of the band he had never had a serious girlfriend; Nervous Boy let it slip that he had never eaten chocolate; Mind-Reader proudly announced that he hadn't gained an ounce since the age of thirteen; and Mystery Boy informed them that he had lost his virginity at age eleven. As for the journalist, she completed her earlier answer by explaining that she had gotten her job as a junior reporter by nepotism. None of the other members of the tiny group (which had now grown to include the journalist as well) were satisfied with the few secrets they'd shared so far, so they continued the game. Their answers became more and more sinister, reflecting their innermost feelings and exposing everything they had worked hard to keep hidden.

A few hours later, the journalist had to leave. She got into her car, drove out a few miles and then carefully removed her wig and make-up. When she reached office, she was greeted by her friend and colleague, who was junior to her.

'How did it go, boss?' she asked.

'Pretty well. We played a little game. It was quite revealing and in fact better than what I had planned. I told you how foolish they are. They practically volunteered the information.'

'And?'

'Well, George tries to hide his depression behind a mask of cheerfulness and sociability; Lachlan's nervous air is not due to anorexia as most believe, but because he's gay—it caused quite a stir among his bandmates; Milo is somewhat of a mind reader and read me right—he said I had blinding ambition, but he also made the mistake of saying I was nice; as for the ever-charming and mysterious Colin, he didn't remember me and tried to flirt with me again. He also confirmed that he might have misbehaved with some girls. Anyway, I have it all on tape. I think I have more than enough information for my scathing exposé.'

'What did you give them in return?'

'Bullshit, of course. I told them I had never been to college.'

'And they bought it?'

'They think I got my job as a supposedly junior reporter through nepotism. Just goes to show you what some people will believe. To think they were my favourite band before the Colin incident. I was almost excited to meet them again. Now look at me! Simultaneously exposing them for the bilge rats they are and launching my career and magazine. The Academy will think twice before giving them another Grammy, while their adoring fans, seeing them for who they really are, will abandon them, just like I did.'

'It seems our hard work has paid off, Annie.'

'It seems it has.'

Radar

I always warned the boss when I sensed someone was shifty. In our business, this was an invaluable skill which the boss appreciated. He admired my loyalty to him. Based on my assessment of a new supplier, the boss would either accept him quickly or grill him about his other customers. As his Assistant Manager/Sometimes Carpenter, the boss relied on me to keep him safe and I always did. Until that particular Tuesday when the Fates conspired to make me doubt that my inbuilt radar, that had successfully detected scoundrels and cheats for years, was wrong. And it was terribly distressing. By the way, I don't know if I mentioned that my boss owns a furniture store.

The man who befuddled my judgement had offered his services as a supplier of furniture varnish. He introduced himself as Mr Sharma. That was the first thing that set my alarm bells ringing. Sharma is the Smith of India—one of the most common last names in existence. I closely observed him as he walked around the store and oh-so-innocently examined the woodwork of a particular table I had produced.

'I love this!' he exclaimed. 'The craftsmanship is beautiful! It will bring you great profit!'

My poor boss, the naïve man that he is, actually mistook the blatant act of flattery for praise.

'You are very kind, sir,' my boss said, beaming at him, 'but in fact he,' he paused to point at me, 'he is the genius carpenter behind this work of art.'

My boss was far too benevolent. However, with such good-naturedness there also came excessive faith in this man who was clearly up to something. I could see that he implicitly trusted the stranger and would have, metaphorically speaking, traded him magical beans for an ordinary cow. This man intended to deceive my boss out of his hard-earned money, but he was not going to have any of it. Not if I could help it.

'Tell me, Mr Sharma,' I said haughtily, 'have you come to sweet-talk us or sell us varnish?'

My boss was shocked, but Sharma was unfazed. In fact, he laughed heartily.

'Well,' he finally said, 'you certainly seem eager to get down to business. In that case, let us not waste any more time. Please give me some spare wood to demonstrate this magnificent varnish.'

'Certainly,' my boss answered.

We walked across the busy street and into the narrow alley where our workshop was. Crouching around a small coffee table they were making were two other carpenters, Rahul and Dinkar. When they saw us come in, they stiffly greeted all three of us and continued doing their work. My boss retrieved a plank of wood for the salesman to demonstrate the 'wonder' of his supposedly exceptional varnish. He smugly applied some to the wood and pointed to it proudly. The colour was a beautiful dark mahogany. It was a rich and stunning shade with an excellent finish. Not at all what I had expected from a man I was convinced was a phoney. A tiny voice nagged me. 'Face it,' it said, 'your radar is not what it used to be.' Immediately I banished the voice from my head and snapped back to reality. It was not pretty, for it involved standing by watching my boss enamoured by the varnish and offering to splurge a large amount of money on it. Mr Sharma seemed a little too self-satisfied by the reaction generated by his varnish, increasing my suspicions. He grinned smugly as my boss raved on and on about how much he loved the varnish.

Back at the shop, Mr Sharma and my boss animatedly discussed rates for the varnish, while I carefully observed the slimy stranger. Eventually, it became too much for me and I had to pull my boss aside to share my fears with him.

'Is everything all right?' the boss hissed. 'I was about

to close the deal.'

'Boss...'

'What is it?' he asked, his face wrought with concern.

'Boss, I don't trust Mr Sharma.'

'Why not? Is it your radar?' he asked.

'Yes,' I replied.

The boss sighed.

'Look,' he began, 'I implicitly trust your radar most of the time, but this is perhaps the one time you may just be wrong. You saw the quality of the varnish he brought. How can any one swindle us with a varnish that good? As for the price, I think I'm smart enough not to let him con me.'

'True enough boss,' I said, 'but I still think he is suspicious.'

Suddenly, I had a brainwave.

'Boss!' I cried (as softly as possible), 'I can follow him to see if he's up to anything.'

'Are you crazy? You do know that stalking is a criminal offence? I will not allow you to do it.'

'But boss! If I can prove—'

'You will prove nothing! I can't allow you to stalk someone like that!'

That ended it. I went and sat in a corner and sulked while my boss and the Slimeball continued to argue about the price of the varnish. It was eight o'clock when they finally stopped. However, they hadn't reached an agreement, they simply decided to postpone their haggling to the next day. Mr Sharma left, and I did too while my boss stayed behind to lock up. As I walked to my motorbike, I realized that my boss was not watching me. I could in fact tail Mr Sharma and see what he was up to. I quickly started up my bike and cautiously rounded the corner to follow his silver car. Through the car's wing mirror I could see the elongated shape of Mr Sharma's head. He drove like a madman, making it hard for me to keep up, but I always managed to keep the silver car with the Haryana plates in sight. He headed into a more dangerous part of town, but I still followed him. Finally, he came to a halt in front of a construction site. Intrigued, I whipped out my cell phone to record what he was up to. To my astonishment, he took out a bucket and spade from his back seat and started shovelling mud from a mound. Feeling utterly bewildered, I watched him labour at it for ten minutes. Then he proceeded to open the boot of his car and remove two large cans of what seemed to be glue. He fetched a bucket of water from somewhere close by and poured it into the glue. I watched in horror as he then dumped the mud into the mixture. I had been right. Mr Sharma was a fraud.

The next day, I described what I had seen to my boss, who was at first angry that I had disobeyed his orders. However, when I concluded my tale and showed him the video on my phone, he was even more appalled and flabbergasted than I was. He vowed to break off all business ties with Mr Sharma and to never doubt my radar again. At precisely nine o'clock, Mr Sharma arrived, looking slightly better groomed than the previous day. His uncouth beard had been shaved off and he wore a clean and well-ironed suit unlike the day before. He almost seemed like a different person, but it was clear that his change of appearance was intended to take us in.

'Good morning,' he chirped, 'I'm here about varnish. I understand you wanted to buy some and I real—'

'Yes, about that,' my employer cut him short, giving him a frosty stare, 'my friend here followed you last night after you left here. He was amazed at how you made a mixture of mud and glue you clearly intended to dupe me with.'

'What?' the man exclaimed, looking genuinely taken aback, 'Sir, I don't know what you're talking about! I was at home last night with my wife, and besides, this is my first visit to your store.'

'How dare you try and lie to me after what you tried to do?' my boss screamed.

'SIR! I assure you it was not me!'

'Then who else could have come in here who looked like you? Huh? Your twin brother?'

The man looked like he'd had a sudden realization.

'Did the man who came in here have a beard?' he

asked.

'Yes,' my perplexed boss answered.

'Oh sir, you really have hit upon the truth! That rogue is my twin brother.'

As the three of us discussed the matter further, we realized he was right. He even showed us pictures of him and his brother. Eventually the boss and the new Mr Sharma struck a reasonable deal over the varnish and I was quite pleased when we tested it again and found that it was all right. Mr Sharma brought out two giant barrels of the varnish from the back of his car, which wasn't a silver sedan but a red Sumo. After carefully pocketing an envelope full of cash, he drove away happily.

Meanwhile, my boss instructed me to take the varnish to Rahul and Dinkar in the workshop. I did so and then hung around to watch them use it. After all, we had gone through great pains to get the varnish. Rahul opened a barrel, put a paintbrush in it and was about to spread the varnish liberally over a chair he had been working on, when I stopped him. My radar was going off like crazy. I instructed him to apply it to a spare plank of wood. At first the mixture seemed fine, but then it turned into a goopy, sticky mess. Sharma had duped us. I informed my boss who immediately called the cops. Luckily, Sharma hadn't got too far and they were able to catch him. My boss even got his money back and both he and I learned a valuable lesson: always trust the radar.

Best Friends Forever

D^{*ing-dong!*}

The doorbell resonated across the house, immediately rousing its owner from her afternoon nap. 'I'll get it,' she mumbled sleepily, before remembering that she was the only person in the house. Gone were the days when Amina had shared a house with her family. Now she had moved to a new city with a new life and a new apartment and new-found loneliness. Still, she did wish that in an alien city, someone familiar would re-enter the picture that was her life. She opened the door hoping that her wish had come true, but was disappointed to find it was a courier delivery man. As she signed and received some boring and grossly inflated bills, Amina heard a squeal. Her childhood best friend, Hayali, was standing right behind the man, clutching her bag. Her smile was warmer than the sun.

'Amina!' she screamed before grabbing and pulling her into a hug.

'Hayali!' Amina shrieked.

Meanwhile, the delivery man made a quick and quiet departure from the scene.

Amina immediately ushered Hayali inside and took her bags up to the spare room. Then they settled down on the sofa in the living room to chat.

'Hayali, I haven't seen you since I was nine years old! I know you moved away, but you could have told me that you were leaving,' Amina complained.

'I am truly sorry about that, but our move was very sudden. None of us were able to tell anyone.'

'Well, that doesn't matter. You're here now.'

'Indeed I am.'

'So how long are you here for?'

'All ready to kick me out, I see?' Hayali said, grinning wickedly.

'Not at all!' Amina cried.

'I know, I know. I might be here for a while, I don't know...' Hayali's expression darkened. 'I just broke up with my boyfriend and I've been feeling very lonely, so I thought I'd visit you,' Hayali said, the words coming out in a rush.

'I know a thing or two about loneliness myself,' Amina said. 'I've lived with my large family for a long time, but now I live alone in this humongous city. Sometimes, I feel completely isolated.'

'It's okay buddy,' Hayali said, affectionately patting Amina's shoulder, 'we have each other now.'

'Yes, we do.'

The two girls had a wholesome lunch, before deciding to go to the supermarket to get supplies for dinner. At the supermarket, Amina found that she was doing all the work.

'If you've come along, I expect you to help, Hayali,' she said huffing.

'I can't!' Hayali wailed. 'I can't identify good quality vegetables and I'm so indecisive that I can't choose drinks either!'

'Hayali, how do you survive?' Amina joked.

'Fast food is forever. Plus, my boyfriend used to do all the cooking.'

Amina saw her friend's bottom lip tremble.

'It's all right, Hayali,' she said, 'it's all right.'

The two of them finished shopping and headed back home, not noticing the disapproving looks they were getting from the other customers.

The next morning, Amina came down to find Hayali already dressed and sitting on the sofa in the living room.

'Sleep well?' Amina asked, rubbing the tiredness out of her eyes.

'Yup,' Hayali answered cheerfully.

'Good, good. I'm going to whip up some pancakes.

You do like pancakes, right?'

'I think you've forgotten, Am, that we always ate the same things. Whatever you like, I like too.'

'That is true,' Amina said, smiling.

At breakfast they discussed the day's itinerary, which involved frequent assurances from Amina that she did in fact have time to spend with Hayali. The two of them decided to catch the latest flick from their favourite director. The movie was your typical romantic, cheesy chick flick, but the girls loved every minute of it. They were thoroughly disappointed when it paused for the interval; however, the hiatus did come at a fortuitous time as Hayali needed to use the bathroom.

'I'll be back in a jiffy!' she exclaimed before running off, leaving Amina laughing.

While the ads were playing, a man came up to Amina and asked if he could take the seat next to her.

'Sorry,' she responded politely, 'my friend has this seat.'

'I normally wouldn't ask,' the man apologized, 'but the person in front of me is far too tall. Anyway, I'm sorry I bothered you.'

'It's all right.'

Just as the movie started, Hayali returned to her seat and both girls focused on the movie. They didn't notice the man a few rows behind them who looked suspiciously at the seat he had requested to sit in.

A few days later, Amina and Hayali decided to go out

for lunch. However, there was one big problem hindering their choice of restaurant—Hayali's indecisiveness.

'Let's go to a Mexican place,' Hayali exclaimed, eyeing a Tex-Mex restaurant.

'No!' she piped up two seconds later. 'How about McDonald's?'

In the course of two minutes, Hayali came up with five different cuisine options including Turkish, Japanese and French along with more mainstream choices. When Amina asked her to decide on one, Hayali told her that she herself would not eat and that the restaurant options were for Amina. When they finally sat down in the Turkish place, both had a hearty laugh about the misunderstanding. Neither of them noticed the strange looks the restaurant's customers and patrons were giving them.

Over the next few weeks, Amina and Hayali spent countless hours in each other's company. The constant laughter and happiness around the house was infectious. Amina slowly felt her loneliness ebb away.

One day, Amina and Hayali decided to do a bit of shopping. While Amina picked up tons of clothes, Hayali trailed after her, looking longingly at them. Amina happened to notice this.

'Why aren't you looking at stuff, Hay? Do you want to go home?'

'No... I just don't have any money for these clothes.'

'I'll pay for you.'

'No! I won't let you! Besides I can't find anything I like.'

'Then, do you want to go home?'

'I already answered that,' Hayali said angrily, 'stop pushing.'

'Hayali, we are here so that *you* can enjoy yourself!' Amina responded irately, her voice rising.

'People are staring, Amina. Come on,' Hayali hissed.

They moved away from the shop and were walking towards another one when Amina noticed something strange. She and Hayali were not shouting anymore, but people were still gawking at them.

'Hayali, I think we better cut this shopping trip short. Everyone is watching us,' she whispered.

Hayali nodded.

The two of them headed to the car wordlessly and drove off. However, their earlier conversation in the store was still fresh in Amina's mind, and as the hostess she felt duty-bound to ask her friend whether she was being properly taken care of or not.

'Hayali,' she began, her eyes still firmly trained on the road as she drove, 'am I really pushing you too much to do things you don't want to do?'

'Yes,' Hayali replied, her lips set in a firm line.

'Oh Hay! Why didn't you tell me earlier?'

'Don't get me wrong, Amina. I love movies, but

shopping isn't really my thing.'

'Then why didn't you tell me?'

'Because you were happy that you didn't have to do things alone.'

Amina was touched by Hayali's words.

She turned to face her, but the split second of diverting her attention from the road took its toll.

'Look out!' Hayali screamed, her face contorted with terror.

Her warning was in vain; the car swerved to avoid an oncoming motorbike and crashed into a nearby ditch. There was a deafening roar as the bonnet slammed into a tree. Soon, passers-by gathered and someone informed the police and a hospital of the accident, the rest of the crowd tried to retrieve the solitary figure in the midst of the wreckage.

∽

Amina awoke in the hospital and was immediately startled by the stark white environment she was in. The nurse on duty fetched her parents, who were overjoyed to see their daughter alive and well. They reminded the scared and confused Amina about her accident and it was only then that she remembered Hayali.

'Where is the other girl who was in the car with me?' she asked breathlessly.

Her parents looked puzzled.

'What other girl, Amina?'

'My friend Hayali.'

'Hold on, I'll just ask,' Amina's mother said, and went to catch hold of a nurse.

Amina's father simply held her hand tight.

A few minutes later Amina's mother and the nurse returned.

'Ma'am, there was no other person with you,' the nurse said placidly.

'But there was!' Amina cried. 'You have to find Hayali!'

'Ma'am, believe me, there was nobody else in the car.'

Amina couldn't believe it. Perhaps Hayali had escaped from the car before the accident, but Amina didn't want to leave anything to chance. She decided that once she was discharged from the hospital, she would go down to the police station and file a missing person's report.

That night at the hospital, Hayali made an appearance in Amina's dreams.

'Because you were happy that you didn't have to do things alone,' she said, her last words to Amina echoing throughout Amina's dream.

Amina suddenly awoke. She was surprised to see Hayali in front of her, completely unscathed.

'Hayali, what are you doing here?' Amina demanded. 'How are you unharmed?'

'Oh Amina,' Hayali said, smiling dreamily, 'I think

you already know the answer.'

Amina woke up again, this time in reality. The dream was an epiphany. Again Hayali's words in the car rang in her ears.

'Because you were happy that you didn't have to do things alone.'

Amina realized that Hayali was truly the best friend she would ever have. Twice Amina had been lonely and twice Hayali had shown up. Hayali had been someone to alleviate the solitude. She had always had Amina's best interests at heart, how could she not? Hayali was a figment of Amina's imagination, her imaginary best friend.

The Conversation

'Thank you for coming at such short notice.'
'No, it's no problem at all.'
'I'm glad. Mrs Sinha, it's serious.'
'Why, what happened?'
'He has killed again.'
'Oh my goodness!'
'Yes, Mrs Sinha, it is shocking, but we need your support at this time.'
'Of c-course. Anything I can do to help.'
'Did you observe Rohit last evening? What was he doing?'
'I saw him in the garden last evening. He was just sitting there.'
'I see. Was his behaviour anything to be concerned about?'
'Didn't seem to be at the time. You know how it is.

Hindsight is 20-20.'

'Of course. That it is.'

'Oh God, but I should have seen this coming! I should have realized he would revert to his old habits and never change! This is all my fault!'

'Mrs Sinha, he had us all fooled. Not just you.'

'But I was right there! I should have noticed something was off!'

'What was off?'

'Well, he was quiet at dinner. Rohit is always quiet at dinner, but I'm pretty sure he was quieter than usual. Now that I think about it, it's almost like he knew he had done something horrible.'

'Mrs Sinha, I'm afraid there is one piece of information that makes things worse.'

'Oh dear.'

'He was seen eating the body.'

'What?! T-t-that can't be right!'

'I'm afraid it is.'

'L-Like I told you last time. I know he kills. And now it seems that killing has graduated to eating! H-how could Rohit do this? Your witness must be m-mistaken.'

'I'm afraid not. She is severely traumatized, Mrs Sinha. We have no reason to doubt her. The fact remains that your son is wreaking havoc on the playground. First, he kills butterflies in front of sensitive children and now he is eating them!'

'I know, Principal Singh. I've told him before. I should have realized that his silence equalled guilt. He knew what he was doing was wrong as I have told him so before, but I guess I will have to enforce the lesson again. I am not sure how much harsher the punishment can be for a five-year-old.'

'That is between you and your son, Mrs Sinha, but I have to address the concerns related to my school and I cannot have Rohit chewing butterflies in front of the other children, who adore them. It can be quite traumatizing for them.'

'I'm sorry. Don't w-worry, I'll take care of it.'

'Thank you, Mrs Sinha, and my secretary has a glass of water outside, I hope your hiccups settle down.'

'M-me too, sir.'

Diamond in the Rough

Minisha glanced at her phone and saw the notification pop up for a new text message.

'Come to the woods tonight. The place you and your twin sister go to.'

The message was extremely odd since Minisha didn't have a boyfriend; nor had she ever told anyone about their secret place. No one except her sister knew of it. Moreover, the text was from an unknown number. Feeling extremely worried, Minisha texted back asking the person to identify themselves. The response that arrived half a minute later shocked her.

'What do you want?' she typed back, fingers trembling.

'The stone.'

Minisha grabbed her jacket and the stone. She ran downstairs and out of her apartment building. Her phone was in her pocket with the message open: a photo of

Minisha's sister, Mona, tied to a chair, facing a masked man who was pointing a gun to her forehead.

She jumped into her car and the tyres squealed as she sped off. Her mind was racing, desperately trying to figure out who had her sister. The kidnapping was obviously an attempt to get something Minisha and Mona had accidentally stumbled upon the previous year.

Last summer, the siblings had gone to visit their grandmother in the pokey old town that she lived in. Like all visitors to the town, they were also told stories about jewels buried in that area. As a joke, the sisters had dug up the ground around their grandmother's house in search of the jewels. They had expected to hit the jackpot in terms of tin cans, but instead found something better. They had found that the rumours were true. At the time, neither Minisha nor Mona had known exactly what to do with their find. However, it did bother Minisha that an uncut diamond of an astronomically high value was lying in their shared apartment. Currently though, Minisha was puzzled that anyone even knew about the diamond. They had kept it a secret from their friends and family, including their genial grandmother.

As she drove, she tried to figure out who she might be dealing with. The kidnapper was clearly someone who was smart and knew their routines. That was the only way he could have abducted Mona.

Minisha finally reached the forest. She scrambled to

the spot she was looking for and quickly dug with her bare hands and buried the diamond in the ground. She covered it up, patted down the soil and ran to the best spot in the forest. Her sister had found it a few years ago; a quiet, beautiful place under an ancient tree.

She waited there for a few minutes wondering if anyone would come, when a black van pulled up. Two large, beefy men wearing ski masks emerged and walked towards her.

'Where's my sister?' Minisha screamed at them.

They didn't answer. Before Minisha could register what was happening, one of them whipped out a cloth stinking of chloroform, grabbed her and stuffed it in her face. Minisha immediately crumpled.

∽

Minisha awoke in a tiny dank cell. Despite feeling groggy, she forced herself up and rattled the bars of her prison. It was hopeless. She desperately glanced around for Mona and her heart sank when she couldn't see her anywhere. However, her bargaining chip was hopefully still in play, which meant that she had a reasonable chance to save her sister. That is, if her sister was still alive.

A few hours later, Minisha wondered whether anyone had noticed their disappearance. Her cell phone had been taken from her so anyone who had tried to call her more than a couple of times would be worried. However, that was a long shot at best. Her parents didn't call much and neither did her friends. She wondered mournfully whether their normally oblivious neighbours would have realized their prolonged absence.

It was many hours later that the two beefy men finally reappeared. They tied her hands and pushed her along until she reached a windowless room. Inside the room, two dirty old chairs faced each other. They then proceeded to bind Minisha to one of the chairs. A few minutes later another person wearing a ski mask entered the room. This person was much shorter than the beefy men and had a funny rolling gait.

'I'm glad you're finally here, Minisha,' the person said.

Minisha gasped. She would have known that voice anywhere. She had heard it throughout her life, always filled with love and affection. That is, up until today.

'Granny?'

'Ah, so you've figured it out, my dear,' Minisha's grandmother said, unmasking herself.

'B-but why? Why would you kidnap us? Your own granddaughters?'

'Minisha, you speak as if I have deceived you when in fact it is you who has deceived me!' her grandmother screamed.

'What did I do, Granny?' Minisha cried.

'You found a huge diamond on my property. You really thought I wouldn't notice? I opened both my heart and my home to you girls and neither of you thought to include me in your little plan?'

'What plan!?'

'Well obviously you two were planning to sell it and split the profit. Not once did you think of mentioning it to your dear old grandmother.'

'Granny, we aren't trying to sell i—'

'Don't toy with me, girl!' Minisha's grandmother bellowed. 'Now where is it?'

'Granny, we were unsure about what to do with the stone! That's why we didn't tell you!'

Her grandmother pulled out a gun and aimed it at her.

'Enough talk,' she said coldly. 'It's not on your person, so take me to it.'

'But what about Mona?'

'You'll see her after you give me the diamond.'

'She's my sister, Granny. Let me see her. She's my family.'

The old woman's eyes softened briefly.

'All right,' she said.

The two beefcakes returned and led Minisha, shackles and all, down a narrow tunnel. Her grandmother followed closely behind.

They stopped in front of a similar cell in which a girl sat with her back to them. Minisha could tell that her spirit was near breaking point.

'Mona!' Minisha screamed.

Mona immediately turned around.

'Minisha!' she shrieked, darting across the length of her cell and rattling the bars. She then saw her grandmother pointing a gun at her sister and her face turned white.

'You see, she's alive,' their grandmother said dispassionately. 'Now, give me the stone.'

'Granny?' Mona asked bewilderedly, clearly clueless about the situation. 'What's going on here?'

'We take her with us, Granny. She needs to be there,' Minisha said boldly.

To her surprise her grandmother actually agreed to take Mona along. The twins were bound and dragged into the van. Minisha gave her grandmother and the beefcakes directions to where she had hidden the diamond. As they drove to the spot, Minisha mentally debated the pros and cons of giving away the diamond.

When they finally reached the spot, Minisha dug up the diamond.

'Here,' she said, handing it to her grandmother, 'now let us go, Granny.'

'Should I?' her grandmother mused, fingering the diamond, 'No. Betrayal deserves punishment, my dear.'

With that, she fired the gun.

Minisha awoke in a cold sweat. She immediately got up and checked to see if Mona was in the apartment. She was, sleeping soundly. Then she quietly took out the diamond from the safe.

Minisha got into her car and drove until she reached a lake. She looked at the huge diamond one last time before flinging it into the water. She headed back to her car, feeling satisfied. In a black van parked nearby, an elderly lady watched Minisha drive away.

Thoughts

'Shiv, don't forget to bring back all your homework today.'

'I won't, Ma,' Shiv answered, rolling his eyes.

He headed out of the door and walked to school.

It was a Monday, the dreaded day that signified the end of the glorious weekend and the beginning of another dreary week of school. For Shiv, it was worse as he had nothing to help him get through school. Some people had their friends, while others had patience, but Shiv had neither. He often sat alone and spent his classes trying and failing to listen to the teachers. To make matters worse, he had a crush on a girl who would never like him back. Shiv considered Aisha beautiful in every way possible, but he was too shy to talk to her. High school was pure torture for him.

This Monday promised to be just like all the others

gone by. Shiv moped to school, was ignored by his classmates and forced to endure lessons about things he presumably would never use in real life. On his way back from school, he was busy feeling sorry for himself when he noticed a packet of gumdrops lying on the pavement. It seemed unopened. Normally, Shiv would have left it lying on the road, but he felt inexplicably drawn to it and despite himself picked it up, examined it and found that it was indeed an unopened packet. He opened it, took out a gumdrop, popped it into his mouth and put the rest into his bag.

In a few minutes, Shiv reached home. He put his schoolbag away and went in search of his mother. He found her napping in her room. He was just about to exit when he heard a soft murmur. It sounded like his mother's voice.

'Yes, Ma?' he said.

His mother didn't respond. After all, she was asleep, what could she have said? He turned to leave when this time he heard a sharp cry. Frightened, he looked at his mother and found that she was indeed in deep slumber. He left the room, concluding that the voice he had heard was probably just the wind outside.

Feeling thirsty, Shiv went to the kitchen and finding no glasses on the shelf, asked the maid to wash one for him. While she was washing it, he swore he heard her grumble, 'This kid is increasing my workload.'

'Excuse me?' he snapped.

'What?' the maid said, looking bewildered. 'I didn't say anything.'

She finished washing the glass and handed it to him. He thanked her and as she smiled at him, he heard her say, 'I hate working in this house.' What alarmed him was not that she had been impertinent, but that her lips had not moved at all. That was when he realized that he had been hearing her thoughts.

Shiv immediately sprinted down to the park in his apartment complex. The nearer he got to the park, the louder the voices got. And when he finally reached the park, the voices were so loud that he was forced to back away to a safe distance. He could clearly hear every child's thoughts. Shiv suddenly realized how much fun he could have with his new-found power.

The next day he went to school feeling much more relaxed, even happy. He spent his classes listening to everyone's thoughts. The teacher was surprised when he immediately answered a question that was designed to catch him off-guard. It was easier to swipe answers off a brainiac's thoughts. He was able to actually talk to people without fearing what they thought of him. All he had to do was listen closely. His only regret was that he hadn't been able to try out his powers on Aisha, who hadn't come to school that day.

Shiv expected to hear a burst of chatter when he got

to school the next day. However, the halls of the school, despite being crowded, seemed to be much quieter. The voices were still audible, but definitely softer. Shiv almost couldn't hear them at all. As much as he tried, he could only catch snippets of thoughts and nothing of substance. By lunchtime, the voices were gone, leaving Shiv dejected. While sitting in class, he was completely miserable as he tried to come to terms with the loss of his powers. It just so happened that during the last lesson he decided to have one of the gumdrops and lo and behold, the voices returned, louder than ever! When Shiv returned home he carefully locked up the remaining six gumdrops in a safe place and went down to the park again just to be certain that he still had his powers.

The gumdrops had truly changed Shiv's life. He was conversing with people so much now that he felt he almost had some friends. He also realized that his fear of what people thought of him had been irrational: while some people thought he was an oddball, there were others who seemed to hold no ill thoughts against him. He even found that some of classmates had similar tastes. Within three days, Shiv's overall popularity skyrocketed.

However, despite all this, Shiv had not yet spoken to Aisha and decided that now was the time to do so. Up until now, his greatest fear had been what she would think of him, but now, that was clearly no problem. Still, he did feel nervous walking up to her, so he decided to stand close to her and listen to her thoughts. Nothing. He moved slightly closer with no success. He moved nearer and nearer until finally he was so close that he ended up bumping into her and apologizing. Even then, he could not hear her thoughts.

The fact that the one person whose thoughts he could not read happened to be his crush, drove Shiv insane. Over the next few days, he desperately tried everything he could to hear a sliver of her thoughts. He sat behind her in class, he ignored the scornful looks thrown his way when he cut the lunch queue to stand behind her, he frequently collided with her in the hallway and jogged the fastest he ever had in his life to try and stay near her during PE.

However, his best efforts proved to be futile. Shiv could hear the nerds' brains busily working away, the sports freaks' minds wander to the field during lessons, the songs stuck in the heads of music lovers and the thoughts girls had when they giggled with each other. None of this was enough because he couldn't hear Aisha's thoughts. She was the only one whose innermost contemplations he badly wanted to hear.

As the days went by, Shiv consumed the remaining gumdrops until finally there was only one left. The day he popped the final gumdrop into his mouth was ironically a Monday again, two weeks after he had discovered his powers. Shiv was feeling extremely morose. Today was his very last chance to discover what Aisha thought of him and perhaps, it was the very last chance for him to talk to her. Afterwards, he'd probably be too nervous to approach her again. At school, he took his usual place behind her and tried hard to get a glimpse into her mind. To his surprise, she turned around to face him.

'Hi Shiv. Are you okay? You've been acting a bit weird lately,' she said.

'Yes, yes! I'm absolutely fine! Completely fine!' he blabbered, amazed that she was even talking to him.

'About your stalking me...'

He was shocked.

'No, Aisha I would nev—'

'No Shiv. You have been stalking me this week trying to hear my thoughts. Haven't you?'

'H-how did you know?'

'Simple. I can't hear your thoughts either. Till last week everything was fine and now it's not. It isn't a coincidence that I haven't been able to access your thoughts since the day I lost my packet of gumdrops. The effect of both of us chewing them cancels out our abilities to read each other's thoughts. The maker of the gumdrops intended for me to use the power to help others and now I have to help you, Shiv, for your own good...'

'I-I-'

Unlike Shiv who was bewildered, Aisha pursued her questioning.

'Do you have any left?'

'N-no.'

'All right then, come with me.'

She walked out of the classroom and Shiv, wordlessly and without even knowing what he was doing, followed her. She led him to a remote corner of the school and then handed him another gumdrop.

'Right, have this.'

Without considering the consequences, Shiv popped the gumdrop into his mouth. As he chewed it, he began to feel his brain slowing down and the voices he had gotten used to quieting down. Finally, after about a minute or so, they ceased altogether. But along with the voices, his memories of the last fortnight were gone too.

He felt dazed as he looked around him and saw that he was in the corner of the school grounds, what was he doing here? And what was Aisha doing with him? He was so confused that he forgot he was afraid of talking to Aisha and asked her what was happening. She replied nonchalantly that he had been going up to class and they were simply heading in the same direction. Back in class, Shiv found the lesson immensely boring. It made matters worse when he realized that it was just another monotonous Monday.

Prized Possessions

'Rina! Get up na! I can't find my lip gloss anywhere! I'm late for my date!' Rina's roommate screamed, yanking everything out of her cupboard. 'Rina! Have you seen it?'

Rina reluctantly looked up from the book she had been so deeply engrossed in, a beautiful leather-bound edition of *Pride and Prejudice*. She was highly amused by the state her roommate was in.

'No,' she drawled, a smile playing on her lips, 'I haven't seen it.'

'Well,' the annoyed roommate announced, 'I'll have to use my other shade of coral! This must be the work of that campus thief!'

She quickly applied the lip gloss and ran out in a huff, slamming the door on her way out. Rina continued to read.

It was half past eight, when Rina started to feel hungry. She put the book away, gathered her things and went for dinner.

In the campus dining hall, she stood quietly in the queue and after two minutes had a dismal plate of dal chawal with bhindi ki sabzi in her hands. She headed over to the table where her semi-friends Minni, Koyal, Nimisha and Ambika sat. They were generally nice to her, especially Minni, but there was always some distance between Rina and the others, not to mention that they had vastly differing interests. While they were outgoing, Rina was extremely shy. While they frequently went on shopping trips, Rina preferred to stay back with her books. And when they went to an amusement park, Rina watched the news. Even though they always invited Rina, she usually made up some excuse not to go—partly because she found it hard to extend conversations and partly because she enjoyed her solitude. They smiled warmly at her as she settled down next to them.

'How are you, Rina?' Ambika asked kindly.

'Fine,' Rina answered without looking up from her plate, 'how are all of you?'

'Good, good,' Koyal replied, with a smile.

After that, the other girls continued their conversation while Rina ate, silently observing them. Some days she wished she could engage in lengthy exchanges like them, but on other days everything they said seemed trivial and frivolous. Rina decided to get some dessert while the others were still chatting. She got a cup of ice cream at the counter and was moving through the crowd towards her table when a boy, busy texting on his iPhone, bumped into her.

'Watch where you're going!' he snapped before walking off unscathed; meanwhile the ice cream had splattered all over Rina, leaving stains on her favourite shirt. She got a tissue and wiped it off, but the cold sticky stain spread. When the others at her table saw the state of her shirt, they made sympathetic noises, which Rina found slightly irritating. She excused herself to go and change, walking past everyone towards the door, when Minni pulled her aside.

'Did you complain against your roommate yet?' she asked, her eyes full of concern.

'No,' Rina answered flatly.

'Rina, you know as well as I do, what she's doing is wro—'

'There's no point, Minni. She'll only blame me for tattling on her. I shouldn't have told you and now, I need to change my shirt.'

At that moment a loud scream of anguish was heard across the hall. Everyone gathered around its source—the texter Rina had collided with. He was really agitated and as people tried to pacify him, they found out he had lost his prized phone. Rina however, took the opportunity to slip out. As she glanced at the crowd behind her, she swore she saw her roommate near the door.

Rina walked briskly back to her room and changed her shirt. Opening her drawer, she was relieved to find her prized possession, her Austen, still there. She buried herself in Elizabeth Bennet's world.

A few minutes later, there was a knock on the door. It was Rina's roommate.

'Weren't you supposed to be out longer?' Rina asked nervously.

'Yes,' the roommate replied, shoving her aside and walking in, 'but my idiotic boyfriend forgot about the date, so I just went to the dinner hall and ate. It's probably for the best, given that I can't find my best coral lip gloss. I wouldn't want to dress down for him.'

'Certainly not,' Rina said, turning back to her book.

'Hey, did you hear about the commotion in the dining room? Rakesh lost his phone! The poor boy must be so lost without it. It's that damn thief *again!*' the roommate chirped away. Normally Rina just ignored her, but the thief was of particular interest to her. She knew far more about the matter than she let on. When the conversation finally let up, she went to bed and dreamt of life in Austen's golden era.

Thump! Thump!

Rina woke up in a panic. The moment she dreaded every night was here. She glanced over at the nightstand—

two o'clock. The thumping noises came again and she squeezed her eyes tightly shut. She heard a new sound now, the shuffling of footsteps in the direction of the window. Rina opened her eyes ever so slightly, just in time to see her roommate throw open the window and embrace the man coming through it—her boyfriend.

'Sorry I'm late,' he whispered.

'Well, sorry doesn't cut it. I should leave you hanging, the way you left me tonight. Now, quick, let's get out of here so we can go to your room.'

With that, the two stepped onto the ledge outside and disappeared. Rina watched them go with disgust. It had bothered her for many weeks that her roommate spent the nights in her boyfriend's hostel. The first time it had happened, Rina had been so upset that Minni had noticed and she was forced to tell her. Minni insisted that she report her roommate, but Rina did not want to be labelled a tattler. She had been given many horrible names already in her life and could not bear the thought of earning one more. However, her roommate's absence did give her the chance to do something she would not otherwise have done.

Rising out of bed, Rina threw open her cupboard and felt around at the back. She pulled out an old box and unlocked it. Then she carefully retrieved the iPhone from under her pillow and placed it with the many other treasures in the box—a trinket bracelet, shell combs, wads of cash, Beats earphones and a coral lip gloss. She smiled as she admired her ever-growing collection of things, each a prized possession of those who had wronged her. Then she locked the box and carefully put it back in its hiding place. Finally she pulled out her gorgeous *Pride and Prejudice*, giggled hysterically and began to read.

The Games People Play

'Step up, step right up and try to win the game! It's very simple. I have three cups and under one of them is a mysterious and beautiful jade. Find the stone and it's yours to keep,' the man behind the counter proclaimed loudly to the awestruck crowd around his stall.

'My name is the Djinn and I promise you my game is 100 per cent genuine,' he continued, 'if all of you will line up, I'll give each of you a shot at the jade, but first let me show you the prize.'

From under one of the red cups, the Djinn pulled out a perfectly cut and smooth stone. The sunlight reflecting from its green surface made it look even more beautiful. There were a few 'oohs' in the crowd—music to the Djinn's ears. He carefully placed the stone back under the cup and then shouted, 'Are you ready to win this?'

'Yes!' came the deafening and unanimous roar.

'Then let's begin!' the Djinn bellowed.

A long line grew in front of the Djinn's counter. Over the next four hours, people tried and failed to earn the coveted stone under the cup, until finally a man in the middle of the queue exclaimed that the game was rigged. His outburst caused most of the people to fall out of the line, but the Djinn didn't care. He attended to the remaining customers, until they too dispersed, grumbling about their stupidity for falling prey to such a cheap scam.

Once everyone was gone, the Djinn gathered up his things and headed to his battered, second-hand car, where he met his teenaged son.

'How much did you make?' the Djinn asked.

'Enough. The crowd was even more distracted tonight,' the son replied with a smile, pulling out a dozen wallets from the pockets in his jacket. 'What about you?'

'Quite a bit, son,' the Djinn said, pulling out a thick wad of cash.

They were about to drive off when they heard a police car siren and a cop signalled at them to pull over.

'God,' the son muttered as the police officer walked up to their car.

'Licence,' he said dispassionately.

The Djinn immediately retrieved his licence from his wallet and handed it over. He also flashed the cop as bright a smile as he could muster for good measure.

The officer closely examined the licence. He had

observed the Djinn's performance and knew he had earned a significant amount of cash from his game. The officer wanted the better part of this cash to come to him and hence, required some reason for demanding money. He had hoped that the Djinn's licence would be a phoney, but was greatly disappointed when he found it was real. He then began to examine the car and was frustrated when he found it to be in as pristine a condition as was possible for an archaic car.

Meanwhile, the amused Djinn called out, 'Is there a problem, sir?'

The Djinn's son sat nervously in the car. If the policeman decided to search them, he would find the wallets stuffed in his jacket. While his father's money was accountable, the wallets were not.

'Dad, what if he—' the Djinn's son whispered.

'Shh,' his father hissed.

The police officer ignored them. He had found a way to get his money.

'Sir, could you please step out of the vehicle?' the policeman said, trying to hide the grin that was about to break on his face.

'Sure,' the Djinn answered, calm as ever.

His son, however, squirmed in his seat.

The Djinn casually strolled to where the cop stood behind the car.

'What is the problem, sir?'

'Your licence plate,' said the policeman, triumphantly pointing at it. 'It is registered to the state of New Jersey. You are currently in Nevada.'

'I had the car transported from Jersey two days ago.'

'But your licence says your home address is in Las Vegas, so why is your licence plate wrong?'

'I moved to Vegas a month ago, but my car only got transported recently,' the Djinn answered.

Although he conned people for a living, he wasn't fibbing about the licence plate.

'I don't know, sir. You could be lying,' the policeman said smugly.

'What do you want?' the Djinn asked angrily.

'Some of your earnings, that's all,' the cop replied.

When the Djinn learned the cop's intentions, he considered threatening to report him, but held back realizing that given his own track record, the justice system would side with the policeman. He briefly toyed with the idea of killing him, but did not want to set such a precedent for his son. Besides, murder was a messy business. No, there was only one other solution.

'How about a game?' he said to the cop.

The police officer recoiled in disgust.

'I've seen your *exceptional* talents,' he scoffed. 'I know that you will beat me.'

'What if I give you an advantage? I'll tell you how the trick works,' the Djinn said, 'and I won't put in a bit of my money, I'll put it all in. If you win, it's yours for the taking. Not to mention the jade. However, if I win, you leave us alone. That seems fair to me.'

The policeman was overcome with greed. He had wanted some money, but a ton of money was far more enticing. He quickly agreed to the Djinn's conditions.

'Very well,' the Djinn said, leading him into his car. In the back seat, the Djinn organized the cups neatly, while his son watched worriedly.

'All right,' he began, 'the basis of the trick is simple, watch closely.'

The cop focused on the cups in front of him as the Djinn showed him the one under which the jade lay and then shuffled them.

'Which one has the stone?'

The police officer pointed to the cup on the far left. When the Djinn removed the cup, there was nothing under it.

'All right, tell me your secret,' he barked.

'It's simple,' the Djinn smiled, 'I actually have some invisible elastic under my jacket. It is wrapped around the stone. Observe.'

The Djinn unzipped his jacket. He pointed out a thin piece of string in his armhole.

'What does that do?' the cop asked.

'That, my friend, allows me to bring the stone into my sleeve,' the Djinn announced dramatically, 'it is never under the cups and hence, can never be found.'

The police officer was greatly impressed, but delighted at the same time. There was no way the Djinn could beat him now that he knew his secret.

'Officer, I will now give you three chances, just like everybody else. I will take off my jacket for the trick, so that I can't deceive you,' the Djinn announced.

He made a big show of taking off his jacket while the policeman watched him. Meanwhile, in the front seat, the Djinn's son was overwhelmed with anxiety. He watched the policeman carefully.

'All right, let's get started,' the Djinn declared, once he had removed his jacket.

He quickly shuffled the cups. The cop scrutinized his movements, focusing so hard on the cups that he didn't feel a hand slip swiftly in and out of his jacket.

'Right, officer,' the Djinn said with a smile, 'which one is it?'

The policeman immediately pointed to the middle cup and the Djinn lifted it. There was nothing underneath the cup.

'Two more tries,' the Djinn said.

The second time, the police officer stared even harder at the cups, but was still unable to find the stone. He suspected that there was some foul play involved.

'You're cheating!' he yelled.

The Djinn only smiled.

'Not at all, sir,' he said and lifted all three cups to reveal the jade.

'Last chance, officer.'

The cop was now feeling nervous. It would be devastating if he lost all that easy money.

The Djinn jumbled up the cups at a medium pace. The police officer kept his eyes fined on them, mentally picturing the stone under one.

'Your move, officer.'

The cop carefully considered the cups in front of him.

'That one,' he finally said, pointing to the cup on the far right.

The Djinn raised the cup. The stone was not under it.

The Djinn's son began whooping loudly, while the Djinn himself was grinning from ear to ear. The police officer was fuming.

'I won't leave this car till you give me my money,' he growled.

'No, you will leave,' the Djinn's son said calmly. 'I recorded the entire game on my phone. I don't think you want us to show that to your superiors.'

The policeman had no choice but to leave. He got out of the car, but not before making a few threats. As he watched the battered car speed off into the night, the cop put his hands in his pockets. He felt around and found that his wallet was missing.

Meanwhile, the Djinn's son was proudly telling his

father how he had nicked the policeman's wallet. After he finished his tale, he asked the Djinn how he had outwitted the officer.

'Son,' the Djinn said smiling, 'I think it's time I reveal my secrets to you. Take out the cups and the stone.'

The boy did as he was told.

'Now examine the inside of the cups.'

The boy looked into the cups. The first one looked quite normal, and so was the second; it was in the third cup that he saw a piece of Velcro stuck on the inside.

'Velcro?' the Djinn's son asked, utterly confused.

'Turn the stone over.'

The boy did and found a tiny piece of Velcro on the underside of the stone. He stuck it to the inside of the cup and found that it fit very well.

'Dad,' he said slowly, 'does this mean that the string thing was fake?'

'Of course.'

'How did you get the Velcro on the jade to attach to the Velcro on the cup?'

'Years of practice have helped me to tilt the cup at the right angle for the jade to get stuck to it. While shuffling the stone around in the cup, I manage to get it stuck to its inside.'

'But how ever did you happen to have the string in your sleeve?'

'I like to be prepared, son, especially when I know

that cops enjoy preying on people like us.'

The Djinn's son's mouth fell open; awestruck by his father.

'You're a true genius, Dad.'

'Thank you, son,' the Djinn replied as they sped on to the next fair.

After all, there was always someone to con.

A Match Made in Heaven

'Attention passengers, we are now beginning our descent to New Delhi.'

The flight attendant's announcement excited me. After spending a gruelling twelve hours in what my best friend had labelled the 'metal death contraption' (aeroplane), I was definitely ready for terra firma, but what was even better was that I knew my cousin Aastha would be waiting for me. Despite an age gap of five years, we had practically grown up together and knew each other inside out. I fondly recalled how we had played with Barbie dolls and tried (and failed) to braid each other's hair, along with more recent memories like going to a Coldplay concert together. Although we had kept in touch, I hadn't seen her in person since I had moved to America for college. However, this meeting was going to be different: I had come to India for Aastha's wedding.

When I finally got a chance to de-board the aforementioned 'metal death contraption', I quickly retrieved my suitcases from the luggage area and headed to the airport meeting point. It took me no time at all to locate the warm, friendly face of my cousin amidst the crowd of people waiting there. Next to her was a girl of medium build and bronze complexion wearing a flowery dress. My cousin was just as ecstatic to see me as I was to see her.

'Hiiiii!' she squealed as she enveloped me into a hug. The girl next to her just smiled.

Aastha reached for my bag and yanked it along as we walked. She enthusiastically inquired about my life in America and it was only in the middle of the conversation that she realized that she still hadn't introduced me to her companion.

'Where are my manners?' she shrieked. 'Sanya, this is my cousin, Riana; Riana, this is my best friend Sanya.'

'Pleased to meet you,' I said politely.

'Likewise,' Sanya answered with a warm smile, 'Aastha has told me so much about you.'

'I'm glad to hear that,' I said, returning her smile and wondering why Aastha had never mentioned her before.

When we reached the parking lot, Sanya stepped aside to hail a cab and I took my chance to ask Aastha about her.

'Aastha, who is she?'

'Didn't I tell you? She's Sanya,' she said and began to guffaw at her own lame joke.

I rolled my eyes.

'No, I mean...I've never heard of her. You've never mentioned her to me.'

'Haven't I? Well, just to let you know, she's my best friend. I met her in college and she's amazing and awesome, just like me. We clicked instantaneously.'

'Oh okay,' I said calmly. 'I'm just glad she isn't a cyborg.'

'Shut up,' Aastha growled and dragged me to where the cab and Sanya were waiting.

We headed to Aastha's house and I was affectionately welcomed by my aunt, uncle and various other relatives and the groom-to-be. Ashutosh seemed to be a man of few words, unlike my chatterbox of a cousin, and at first it worried me that perhaps Aastha had chosen the wrong man to marry. However, as all the guests sat around and chatted, I noticed how intelligently he made conversation and also the look of love his eyes reserved solely for Aastha.

My aunt began to ask me about how my classes were going, when a loud crash outside the room, followed by a groan, had us all dashing out. The source of the groan was a young man who had evidently tripped and fallen down the stairs. As we lifted him up and plonked him on the sofa, he introduced himself to me as Virat, Ashutosh's childhood friend. After a quick examination for broken bones and many 'are you all rights' it was established that Virat had escaped unscathed from his encounter with the flight of stairs. We then went on to have a grand dinner, which was more like a banquet than a meal and at the measly hour of nine o'clock, I decided to surrender to my jet lag and went to bed.

The next day was the wedding and I awoke to find myself in the midst of absolute chaos as my aunt, uncle and all the other relatives engaged in a mad scramble. Those who weren't running about doing last-minute preparations for the evening were trying to push Aastha into going to the parlour to begin her bridal treatment. She resisted until the relatives became desperate. Although I didn't see Ashutosh anywhere, I assumed he must have been facing a similar situation.

'Riana!' an aunt yelled at me. 'Will you and Sanya please take Aastha to the parlour?'

Within three minutes, hordes of relatives gathered on the spot and threw us out of the house.

'Why on earth did they make us leave so early?' Aastha grumbled. 'My wedding's in the evening, not in the next hour.'

Sanya exploded into laughter.

'They chucked us out because seeing you made *them* feel stressed,' she said in between giggles.

I realized she was probably right. They could not bear to see the bride sitting calmly; it was too much for them. They *wanted* to run around like headless chickens.

Despite the fact that it was only one o' clock, we went to the parlour for our beauty treatments. Ironically, it did last through the afternoon and in fact, we ended up getting late. On top of everything, my scatterbrained cousin had left her wallet at home. I offered to go and retrieve it.

Back home, I ran up the stairs to Aastha's room on the second floor. I entered her room and began rummaging through all the cupboards and drawers in search of the missing wallet. This was in vain and I went in search of Ashutosh to ask him if he knew its whereabouts.

'Hey Ashutosh,' I said, entering his room, 'have you seen Aastha's wallet?'

'It might be here,' he answered, gesturing to the messy pile of clothes and other things on his bed. 'You'll have to hunt for it, Riana. I have to go downstairs and engage with the relatives.'

'All right,' I said.

I dug through the heap of things in search of the wallet. Why Ashutosh couldn't just organize his things properly was a mystery to me. For some reason he just *had* to have everything in a pile and what's more, my idiot cousin was also dumping her things in the same pile! While I was hunting for the wallet, Ashutosh's iPhone pinged. I ignored it, but it pinged again. And again. I picked it up to find Ashutosh, when the message caught my eye: 'Babe make sure you come to my room later.' The number was not Aastha's. Curious now, I unlocked the phone and checked the source of the messages. It seemed to be Virat, whose number, for some reason, had not been saved. Along with the texts were some photos. Of Virat and Ashutosh kissing.

The photos made me feel sick to the stomach. I had nothing against homosexuals, but the idea of my cousin being a safety net for this man was too much for me. I dropped the phone and immediately ran away from the room (I couldn't bear to stand in the room of a liar) and headed downstairs. Luckily on the way down I met my aunt who knew exactly where Aastha's wallet was. I went back to the salon, a debate raging in my mind. *Should I tell her? After all she is due to marry him in a few hours.* However, at the same time I also thought, *Maybe I should just let it be. She does love him.*

When I finally reached the parlour, we quickly paid the grumbling owner and went back home. On the ride back, I was so quiet that Aastha noticed.

'Riana, you look like you've seen a ghost. Are you okay?'

'Yes, I'm absolutely fine,' I said, flashing a fake grin at her.

But I wasn't, not even close. I couldn't stop thinking about what I had stumbled upon and the possible repercussions that would follow whether or not I decided to tell my cousin about it. The battle raging in my mind seemed to be interminable.

At home, both Aastha and Sanya were greatly impressed by the arrangements in place. As soon as we entered the house, the relatives grabbed hold of Aastha and took her to get dressed. Not wanting to disturb anyone, I went to my room and got ready on my own, all the while thinking about how to address my dilemma. It didn't take me long to get dressed and I quickly went down to join the rest. I was engaged in completely inane conversations with some jovial distant cousins when I saw Virat chatting with my aunt. It was too much for me and I finally made up my mind. I had to tell Aastha.

I headed to her room; I could clearly hear Sanya talking to her.

'Aastha, you don't have to do this.'

'Oh, but I do, Sanya. It's the only way my parents will leave the subject of marriage alone.'

'But marrying a gay man?'

Ha, I thought triumphantly, *she knows*!

'It's a desperate measure, Sanya, sure. However, it is better to marry a gay man than a straight one.'

Now I was puzzled. Why would she willingly commit herself to being the wife of a man who could not love her back?

'Aastha, it's a great sacrifice you're making for us.'

'I have to, Sanya. I love you, but I know that most of

those people out there, including my own parents, would turn against me if they knew I was a lesbian.'

'I still can't believe you'd do this for me, Aastha. I love you too.'

Now, it all made sense to me. I quietly made my way downstairs and dutifully waited for the ceremony to begin. There were joyous screams when the groom arrived, but I knew better. The whole evening, I watched as the preliminary wedding ceremonies went off without a hitch. Then it was time for the bride and groom to solemnize their marriage in the presence of the holy fire. I watched them walk around the fire devotedly, while the guests gazed in awe at what seemed to them to be the perfect pair. They were perfect indeed, so perfect together that they had successfully duped the guests into believing that they had eyes only for each other. To the guests, it was nothing short of witnessing the sanctification of a match made in heaven.

Partners

It was a warm summer's day in New York City.

'Ugghh,' Lalita groaned as she drove, 'stupid heat.'

She was relieved when she spotted a Caffeine Kickstart outlet just a few metres ahead. Lalita entered the coffee shop and let the cold air wash over her. She ordered a frappé and seated herself in a comfortable chair in a corner. She looked around at the other customers for a split second before taking out her laptop from her bag and booting it up. She then swiftly connected to the Wi-Fi and started checking her email.

At the other end of the coffee shop, a man sat in front of the window. He seemed to be watching Lalita, whose back was turned to him.

'Target located. Would you like me to seize her?' he whispered into his watch.

'Affirmative,' said the voice in his hidden earpiece.

With that the man stood up and stormed across the coffee shop. He pulled out the gun concealed in his pocket and fired shots in the air. The terrified shrieks and screams confirmed that he now had everyone's attention. He walked towards a petrified child, who had been sitting at the table ahead of Lalita's, and grabbed her.

'NO! NO!' came her desperate mother's screams.

'I have to take her,' the man said calmly, ignoring her. 'Nobody will stop me and nobody will call the police. If you do, not only will the girl die, but so will all of you. I have friends nearby who will not hesitate to track you down and kill you. That's all, everyone. Have a pleasant afternoon.'

He forced the crying four-year-old out the door and into his car, leaving her hysterical mother behind. He strapped the child in and drove away.

Lalita had watched the entire scene wordlessly. Once the gun-toting stranger had departed, Lalita quickly packed up and walked out the door. All the others in the coffee shop were frozen in fear. Except for the mother of the four-year-old girl, who was weeping and fumbling with her phone.

Lalita got into her car and drove off. It was clear that no one would be calling the cops. The kidnapper had threatened everyone quite effectively. However, he hadn't counted on a cop being in the coffee shop. And he certainly hadn't counted on the best cop in her unit tracking him down.

Lalita knew she wouldn't be able to catch up with the car and she needed help to find the child. So she called her partner, a mountain of a man known only by his nickname Pym—a reference to the secret identity of the superhero Giant Man, whom he resembled in height.

'Lalita?' Pym answered on the first ring.

'Pym, where are you?'

'I'm on Third Street. Why? What's happening?' He did a poor job of masking the excitement in his voice.

'I need your help. Come to my apartment, I'll meet you there, but don't tell the rest of the squad.'

'Why not?'

'I'll tell you when I see you.'

With that, she headed home. She was surprised to find Pym already at her doorstep when she got there.

'Come on in,' Lalita said, unlocking the door.

Pym gunned for the plush sofa near the TV and crashed on it. Lalita settled herself in an armchair more gracefully.

'Right, what's the case?' Pym asked eagerly.

Lalita quickly told him what she had seen.

'All right…' he said slowly after she was done, 'why can't the rest of the police force be involved in a simple kidnapping?'

'It's because of the victim.'

'What about her?'

'Promise me you won't tell anyone about this.'
'You know I won't.'
'Promise me.'
'I promise.'

'All right,' Lalita began, taking a deep breath, 'the girl is called Nicole Benson. She's Malcolm Smythe's daughter.'

Pym was frozen in his seat; the expression on his face was of pure shock.

'Malcolm Smythe? The Malcolm Smythe? The ruthless underground mob boss?'

Lalita simply nodded.

'What the bloody hell! That guy kidnapped Malcolm Smythe's daughter? How is that even possible; and how do you know that's his daughter? They don't even share the same last name!'

'Pym, the name "Nicole Benson" is meant to protect her. If she used her real name, she would be dead by now.'

'Guess I should have realized that.'

'Yes, you should have.'

'Okay...but I still don't understand why we can't involve the rest of the force.'

'Pym,' Lalita said, her face grave, 'the more people involved, the more the likelihood of the girl getting hurt. He said he'd kill her if the cops were involved.'

'But Lalita, why is it so important to get her back to her father?' Pym asked.

Noticing the dirty look she was giving him, he added,

'I mean sure, she's just a kid, but her disappearance might teach Daddy a lesson.'

'Pym, she's an innocent child with a life ahead of her,' Lalita snapped. 'How her father makes a living doesn't matter.'

'Okay,' Pym said reluctantly, 'so how do we find her?'

Lalita's mind began to race. She laid out all the facts. The kidnapper had to have known that Nicole and her mother would be at Caffeine Kickstart that morning. But most people randomly went into Caffeine Kickstart. For someone to have known Nicole was going to be there they would have had to have monitored her movements. Either Nicole and her mother had entered Caffeine Kickstart on a whim, or they were habitual visitors. There was only one way to find out.

She snapped out of her trance to find Pym furiously running a Google search on his laptop. He had had the same thought and was searching for the number of the Caffeine Kickstart branch Lalita had been at that morning.

'Glad to know great minds think alike,' Lalita remarked with a smile.

As soon as Pym found the number, Lalita called it. As the phone rang, she realized it was a long shot that anyone would pick up the phone. After all, there had just been a kidnapping. If nobody picked up then they would have to pay a visit to the outlet again, which would slow them down. Lalita was relieved when the phone was picked up with a shaky 'H-hello?' She would have to play civilian for the barista; announcing herself as a cop was sure to earn a disconnection, given the threats the kidnapper had made about contacting the police.

'Hello, I wanted to know whether you are open this afternoon. I heard you might be shut today.'

'Y-yes we're shut.'

'But you can't!' Lalita wailed. 'I'm a regular, I need my coffee or I'll never be able to finish my humongous report.'

'S-sorry. Go to a-another branch.'

'It's not just me! My neighbour needs his fill too and what about the darling curly-haired little girl and her mother! All of us want this branch to be open!'

'A-all of you can wait and d-don't worry about the little girl. S-she had her hot c-chocolate this m-morning.'

With that the nervous employee hung up.

'So…' Pym said expectantly.

'She seems to be a regular.'

'So he knows where she goes. This was not a random kidnapping. He had been planning it for weeks.'

'With that kind of planning he's probably not alone. It means his motive is either a bounty or revenge. Either way, someone wants Nicole dead. It's got to be someone Smythe is enemies with.'

'Lalita, Smythe has no dearth of enemies.'

'True, but how do we find out which one?'

Pym thought a bit. Suddenly, the answer came to

him.

'Elena,' he thought out loud.

Lalita and Pym hopped into a car and drove to a dank and run-down part of town. They parked Lalita's car nearby and walked up to the homeless woman sitting on the side of the pavement holding a piece of cardboard on which the words 'The End Is Nigh' had been scrawled.

'Elena!' Pym called out as they walked up to her.

Elena saw them coming and scowled.

'What do you want, Pym?' she growled, 'And I see you've brought a friend with you.'

Lalita introduced herself to Elena, but could tell the woman did not care for niceties. They then moved into an alley where they were sure no one would see them.

'Right, down to business,' Pym said, rubbing his hands. 'What do you know about Nicole Benson?'

'Malcolm Smythe's child? Nothing, really,' she said.

Then she smirked.

'Gonna arrest a child, Pym?'

'Do you know of anyone who might have had a beef with Smythe?' Pym continued, ignoring her snide comment.

'Oh, everyone,' Elena said.

'How about recently?' Lalita pushed.

'Recently? Oh, let's see,' Elena said in a mocking tone, 'there was the land tussle with the Italians; the money-laundering business with the Russian family, can't remember their names, the corrupt—'

'Elena! Enough with the smart-assery! Tell us what we need to know! Tell us about the last couple of weeks.'

'All right! Geez! No humour these days! Nothing in the last couple of weeks, although there are whispers about the return of Smythe's greatest enemy.'

'You don't mean...him?' Lalita gasped.

Elena smirked again, evidently pleased at the reaction and attention she was getting.

'Brutus is back in town,' she whispered maliciously.

'This is bad!' Pym exclaimed back in the car. 'This is very bad!'

'This Elena, can we trust her?' Lalita asked.

'She's a treacherous snake, but she needs police help to keep her out of trouble. She's a pretty decent informant.'

'Does she have other police contacts?'

'Nope, just me. Why?'

'Remember, the less people involved...'

'Oh, right.'

'Now,' Pym said after a while, 'it's clear the girl is in Brutus's part of town, but where?'

'I think I know,' Lalita said.

They had driven up to a burned-down restaurant.

'Of course!' Pym exclaimed. 'Brutus would hurt Smythe's daughter at the place that incited their rivalry.'

They drove past the former restaurant, parked at a distance and then slowly went through the back door, each keeping one hand on their firearms.

In the hallway, they noticed two men standing on guard. In silent agreement, both Lalita and Pym pounced on the guards. However, the scuffle was not quiet and attracted the attention of some more of Brutus's lackeys. Completely outnumbered, the cops were grabbed and dragged away. They were taken to the big boss.

'Well hello. What do we have here?' bellowed the large, hefty man in front of them.

He had a scar on one eye and a shiny, clean-shaven head. It was Brutus.

'You won't say? Never mind, I know you're the police and I assume you're here for the girl. I'm sorry, though, I won't allow you to take her. You see, I'm waiting for someone else to come for her.'

'You're waiting for Smythe,' Lalita spat.

'Yes, I am. Thank you for noticing.'

'How do you know that Smythe will know where to come?' Lalita asked.

What is she doing? Pym wondered.

'He'll know,' Brutus said and flashed a grin that displayed his crooked cigarette-stained teeth.

'How do you know he isn't already here?' Lalita questioned.

'What?' the mob boss was confused.

In that second, Lalita capitalized on his bewilderment. She kicked the man holding her and managed to grab his gun from his hands. She had the gun trained on Brutus now.

'Where's the girl?' she demanded.

Brutus didn't answer. He was smiling at the pistol in her hands.

'Where is she?' Lalita roared.

'I see now,' Brutus said slowly, an evil glint in his eyes.

'TELL ME WHERE SHE IS!'

Brutus waved a hand at one of his lackeys. The lackey went off down the hallway and reappeared a few seconds later. He was dragging an unwilling and crying child. It was Nicole.

She saw Lalita and her eyes lit up.

To the utterly perplexed Pym's surprise, Brutus allowed the man to let the child go. She ran up to Lalita and hugged her.

Brutus was still smiling. However, it was not a smile of triumph, but one of bitterness.

'Well played, Malcolm Smythe,' he said, 'but now you d—'

Lalita shot him mid-sentence. He fell to the ground, the evil glint still in his eyes.

As soon as the lackeys realized that their master was dead, they quickly scrammed. Only Lalita, Pym and the child were left.

'What is going on, Lalita? Why was he calling you Malcolm Smythe?' Pym demanded, fear in his eyes.

'I'm surprised you haven't figured it out yet, Pym.'
'W-well, now I sort of have.'
'Try, Pym,' Lalita said calmly.
'There is no Malcolm Smythe. You're the one with the criminal empire, but nobody knows it. That's why you didn't want to involve the squad, lest they figure it out. You have inside information through your daytime job as a cop. You're willing to sacrifice your own child to weed out your enemy. Worst of all, you've been lying to me since the day we first met. Please tell me I'm wrong. Please, please…'

Tears began to stream down his face.

Lalita watched him, her expression empathetic.

'I'm sorry, Pym. Everything is true, except for the part where I sacrifice my daughter. I don't have one. This child was simply a stand-in. She's my niece once removed.'

Pym looked away.

'However,' she continued, her tone soft, 'I haven't been completely dishonest with you. All the fun times we had together were real, but now it's time I say goodbye to you. God knows our friendship was never meant to last.'

She kissed him on the forehead and whispered goodbye.

Then she was gone, walking down the hallway, clutching the child's hand.

Pym realized he should have gone after her. As a police officer it was his duty to arrest crime lords, but he let her stroll right out, scot-free into the night.

Acknowledgements

In no particular order, I would like to thank:

My family, for their endless support in my literary endeavours as well as in everything else I have done.

My friends, Nimrit, Rubaan and Shreya, for always being there for me.

My editor, Ahalya Naidu, for giving me such fantastic inputs and for bringing up miniscule details I tended to overlook.

The team at Rupa Publications, who have worked tirelessly to ensure this book got published on schedule.

My school, The Shri Ram School-Aravali, and all its teachers for providing a nurturing environment brimming with creativity which was my second home for ten years.

And finally, you, the reader.